The Trouble
with Candy

The Trouble
with Candy

Michael J. Pellowski

Hollywood Paperbacks

Printed in the United States of America.
For information, address WBGM Publishing
Company, Inc., 114 Fifth Avenue, New York, New York
10011.

First Edition
1 2 3 4 5 6 7 8 9 10

Library of Congress Cataloging-in-Publication Data
Pellowski, Michael.
The trouble with Candy / Michael J. Pellowski.—1st ed.
p. cm.—(Riverdale High)
Summary: The new girl Candy fears that her perpetual
clumsiness will make her unpopular at Riverdale High,
despite the efforts of her cousin Betty and Betty's
friends to make her feel welcome.
ISBN 1-56282-107-5
[1. Clumsiness—Fiction. 2. High schools—Fiction.
3. Schools—Fiction. 4. Cousins—Fiction.] I. Title.
II. Series: Pellowski, Michael. Riverdale High.
PZ7.P3656Tr 1991 [Fic]—dc20 91-19654 CIP AC

The Trouble
with Candy

Chapter 1

It's not often that something exciting happens in Riverdale. It's a quiet little town, and excitement arrives in small, infrequent doses. Don't get me wrong! Betty Cooper loves Riverdale, U.S.A. I wouldn't trade my hometown for any other place on the map. It's just that in Riverdale, everybody knows everybody else and most of their business, too. Life isn't exactly humdrum, but it tends to follow a routine pattern day after day. I guess that's why Mom's news excited me so. The last time I felt this way was when Riverdale's hottest hunk, Archie Andrews, asked me to the varsity hop at school instead of my friend—and biggest rival—rich girl, Veronica Lodge.

"Betty Cooper, please stop pacing, and sit down," Mom ordered. "You're wearing a path in the middle of the living room carpet.''

"Sure, Mom! Right," I said as I flopped down on the sofa. "Sorry, I'm just anxious. It's been a long time since I've seen Aunt Carol and Cousin Candy."

Mom walked over and sat down beside me. "I know how you feel," she said. "I've missed them, too. With your Aunt Carol, it's always business first. Climbing that corporate ladder sure has kept her busy over the years. Since her divorce, her career has taken her from one city to the next. Putting down roots in Riverdale will be good for her."

I nodded. "I guess moving around is the price you have to pay for being a successful businesswoman," I said. "And Aunt Carol sure is successful. I don't think I've ever met anyone more organized than she is."

Mom threw back her head and laughed out loud, as if at some private joke. "Carol's a real perfectionist," she agreed. "She and I certainly are different."

"Thank goodness for that!" Dad grunted from his chair. He glanced over the top of the paper he was reading and gave Mom one of those meaningful glances.

"Now, Hal, don't start that again," Mom cautioned.

"I'm just kidding, Hon," Dad apologized. "I can't wait to see Carol either. I'm glad her company transferred her back to Riverdale. And it will be especially nice to see Candy." Dad put down the paper and smiled at me. "I used to bounce you two blondies on my knees together," he reminisced.

I laughed. "That was a long time ago," I reminded him. "We've both grown a lot since then. Remember, Candy is four months older than I am and we're both in high school now."

"Thanks for making me feel so old," Dad sighed as he went back to reading his paper.

I leaned my head back against the couch. I wondered what Candy would be like now that she was a teenager. I knew she was attractive from recent pictures she'd sent with her letters. But letters and pictures can't tell you what a person is really like on the inside. I hoped she hadn't changed all that much.

One thing was for sure: Things in Riverdale were going to change now that Candy was moving back home. I would finally have someone I could confide in again. When we were younger, Candy and I had been more like sisters than cousins. Since Aunt Carol had had to work, Candy had spent a lot of time at our house, with Mom babysitting. Candy and I had been so close it almost broke my heart when Aunt Carol was promoted and transferred to New York. But New York had been just the first stop in a long string of cities and promotions for my aunt. I sighed, remembering. That was all behind us now. Candy was finally coming home.

"While you're daydreaming," Mom said to me, "I'll check on the refreshments. Carol should be here any minute."

"If she'd let us meet her at the airport, we wouldn't be waiting around like this," Dad grumbled. "But no! That independent sister of yours has to do everything herself. She goes and rents a car in advance."

"You know how she is," Mom told Dad. "That's why I wasn't surprised when she told me she wouldn't need to stay with us because she'd already arranged to rent a house here in town. Carol likes to have everything under control. That's why she's such a good businesswoman."

"Hmph!" Dad cleared his throat as Mom walked into the kitchen.

"Need some help, Mom?" I asked.

"No thanks," Mom called back. "Everything is ready. Just relax."

"Relax? Right," I answered, settling back on the sofa. Just then the doorbell rang. "They're here!" I squealed, bouncing to my feet. I bolted over to the door, turned the knob, and yanked it open.

Before me stood a meticulously dressed, attractive, middle-aged woman. Her clothes were perfect. Her hair was perfect. Even her makeup was perfect. She looked like she'd just stepped off the front page of a magazine for businesswomen. Beside her was a tall, slender, blue-eyed blonde. I smiled from ear to ear.

"Aunt Carol!" I shrieked as I threw my arms around the lady in the business suit and gave her a big hug.

"Betty! You've grown into a stunning young woman," Aunt Carol complimented, returning my hug.

"Candy!" I cried, transferring my bear-hug hold from my aunt to my cousin. "Welcome home!"

"It's great to be home," Candy answered as we embraced tightly.

5

"Doesn't anyone else get any hugs around here?" Dad asked as he joined us.

"Hal, how are you?" Aunt Carol greeted him. They kissed each other hello. "Sorry we're a little late. We stopped off at our new house to drop off our luggage."

"You're right on time," Dad corrected. He turned to my cousin. "This model beside you can't be our little Candy Girl, can it?" he kidded.

"Uncle Hal, you're still a comedian." Candy pecked a kiss on my Dad's cheek.

"Well, don't just stand in the doorway," Dad said, grinning from ear to ear. "Come in! Come in! Here! Give me your coats. I'll hang them up." Dad took their coats as I ushered Aunt Carol and Candy into the living room.

"Carol! Candy!" Mom cried, racing out of the kitchen with arms outstretched. She hugged both of them at the same time. "It's good to have you home, Sis," Mom said to my aunt. Mom sniffed. Tears welled up in her eyes. I felt tears filling my eyes, too. The feeling was contagious. We were all misty-eyed, except for Aunt Carol. She seemed to have her emotions completely under control.

"What's going on here?" Dad asked

when he returned from hanging up the coats. "Is this a reunion or a funeral? Why is everyone crying?"

"Who's crying?" Mom snapped as she wiped away a tear. "I have a speck of dust in my eye."

"I have a speck of dust in my eye, too," I said.

"Me, too," sniffed Candy.

"Hal," kidded Aunt Carol, "it sounds like your house needs a good cleaning."

"What we need are some refreshments," Mom suggested.

"Sit down, everyone. I'll get them," Dad offered. He headed toward the kitchen.

We went to the sofa and sat down. Almost instantly Mom and Aunt Carol started reminiscing. Candy and I just listened as our moms talked about the good old days. Before long Dad returned with the plate of fancy sandwiches Mom and I had prepared earlier. "I'll be right back with soda for all.

"Here we are," Dad announced as he showed up holding a tray filled with empty glasses and open bottles of soda. He leaned forward and offered us the drinks. Mom and Aunt Carol each took a glass and a bottle of soda. Dad then turned toward Candy and me. As Candy reached for a glass, her hand brushed against a bottle of soda.

"Whoa," cried Dad. He tried to steady the tray but the bottle toppled over, knocking over another bottle as it fell. Ginger ale began to fizz out.

"Yeow!" shouted Dad as foaming bottles rolled off the tray. "Look out!"

Fizzt! Whissst! Upended bottles went sailing everywhere as we ducked for cover. One bottle landed with a loud splat right in the dip. Another hit the platter of sandwiches and sent the tray and the sandwiches flying. The remaining bottles crashed to the floor, sending up geysers of soda that sprayed everyone.

"Eek!" screamed Aunt Carol from under a shower of pop.

When the sudden soda cloudburst finally ended, bottles and food lay in a big mess before us.

"My new suit is ruined," wailed Aunt Carol, dabbing ginger-ale drops off her face with a napkin.

"The klutz curse did it again," I heard Candy murmur.

No one else seemed to hear her remark, so I thought it best to just let it pass. After all, the whole thing was just an unfortunate accident.

"I'm sorry, Aunt Helen," Candy said. "I'll clean it up. I'm really, really sorry. Please forgive me." Her voice was pleading.

"Don't worry about it," Mom said, rising. "I'll take care of it."

"I'll help," Aunt Carol offered as she dabbed at soda spots on her suit with the napkin.

Mom looked at me. "Betty, why don't you take Candy upstairs? After you wash the soda off your faces, show her your room. I'm sure she wants to hear all about Riverdale High. After all, she'll be starting school on Monday."

"On Monday?" Dad questioned. "Carol, why not give Candy a few days off to settle in first?"

"That wouldn't be the efficient thing to do," Aunt Carol told Dad. "It's better to get right at a new job." She looked at my cousin. "Right, Candy?"

"Ah . . . right, Mom," Candy agreed, but not too enthusiastically. I got up and stood beside my cousin.

"Scram, girls," Dad said, shooing us with a wave of his arms. "Get upstairs before you trash the rest of the room." He winked to show us he was just teasing.

"Let's go, Candy," I urged. "I'll fill you

in on all the good-looking guys in school."

"That sounds good to me," Candy said as we started up the stairs to my room. Klunk! Candy stumbled on the second step. I caught her as she fell forward.

"Sorry. I guess I'm a little clumsy today," Candy explained as she regained her balance.

I nodded understandingly. I glanced back into the room where Mom, Dad, and Aunt Carol were starting to clean up the mess. Then I looked at Candy. She was slipping off her high-heeled shoes. "I broke a heel when I stumbled," she said.

I couldn't help thinking about what Candy had muttered earlier. What was the word she used? Klutz? I wondered what she'd meant by that. I tried to put the entire incident out of my mind.

"Come on," I said. "I'll show you where the bathroom is."

"I remember where it is," Candy replied as she shadowed me up the stairs. "I just hope I can reach it without having another accident."

Chapter 2

"Hey! Your room is totally rad!" We had finally entered my inner sanctum after washing off the soda. "Did you decorate it yourself?"

"Of course," I answered. "I call it early art deco mess."

Candy laughed and looked around. She strolled over to my vanity and paused to stare at my favorite photo of Archie. Candy picked up the frame.

"Who's this?" she asked. "Is he your boyfriend?"

"Sort of," I replied. "That's Archie Andrews. Remember him?"

"Archie Andrews?" Candy mumbled. "The name is vaguely familiar. He sure is a hunk. His freckles are cute!"

I blushed. "You don't remember much about Riverdale, do you?" I asked.

"Not really," Candy admitted. "It seems like a million years have passed since I was here last."

"Most of the kids we played with when we were little have moved away," I said. "So you really will be starting over."

Candy smiled at me and nodded. She put the photo back on my vanity. But she didn't shove it far enough from the edge and it toppled onto the floor. Crack!

"Oh no!" she gasped. "Not again!"

Candy lifted Archie's picture off the floor and slowly turned it faceup. I held my breath, then groaned. The glass had shattered into a million pieces. It looked like there were spider webs all over Archie's head.

"I-it's okay," I told my cousin, who was on the verge of tears. "It's no big deal. I can get it replaced."

"*I'm* the thing that should be replaced," Candy said. "It's too bad there isn't a store that sells replacement relatives."

I laid Archie's photograph on my vanity. "Don't feel like that," I said to Candy, putting a hand on her shoulder. "It was just an accident, and accidents happen to everyone."

"They sure happen to everyone around

me," Candy moaned. She flopped down on my bed. "The truth is I'm a jinx! A geek! A complete klutz!"

I was puzzled. "That's the second time I've heard you call yourself a klutz," I said. "You're not a geek and you're not a jinx. Have you looked in the mirror recently? A lot of girls would kill for looks and a shape like yours."

"Oh, right," mumbled Candy. "I look good because I work at it, but I'm a geeky klutz, too, and I don't work at that. I just can't seem to do anything right. I goof up all the time. I break stuff. I trip. I'm just a natural-born, one hundred—proof klutz!"

I sat down beside Candy. "You're over-reacting," I told my cousin. "It's all part of being a teenager. You can't be so self-conscious."

Candy shook her head. "I wish I could believe that."

"Believe it," I coaxed. "I goof up all the time, too. It just seems worse to you because your mom, well, Aunt Carol is so . . . so . . ."

"Perfect," Candy interjected. "She *is* perfect. She never does or says the wrong thing. She's perfect. You can say it."

"Nobody's perfect," I corrected. "She's

just so well organized that next to her anyone would look klutzy."

Candy thought for a minute. She looked up at me hopefully. "Do you really think so?" she asked.

"Of course," I said, trying not to think about the picture of Archie that Candy had just trashed. "Now that you're back in Riverdale, you'll soon forget all about this klutz stuff. You'll see."

"That sounds wonderful," Candy admitted. "I'd like to feel like I've come home to stay. I'd like to finally fit in somewhere." Candy looked wistful. "In the past, I never really fit in at any of the other schools I went to."

"You'll fit in here," I assured Candy. "Archie, Jughead Jones, Veronica Lodge, and all my friends will accept you as if they've known you all their lives."

"Oh, Betty! I hope so!" Candy exclaimed. "It would be so nice to be part of a group, to be popular. You know what I mean. For once, I'd like to be in with the 'in' crowd."

I took Candy's hand in my own. "You will be," I assured her. "Once the guys get a look at you, your phone will never stop ringing."

Candy smiled. Actually, I had a hard

time believing that anyone as pretty as Candy could have trouble making friends—especially boyfriends. Just then Aunt Carol called.

"Candy! Please come down now. It's time to go."

"Do you have to leave already?" I complained. "You just got here."

"That's Mom," Candy explained. "She wants to get settled in as quickly as possible."

"Do you want me to come over and help?" I offered.

"Thanks!" Candy replied. "But not just yet. Mom has her own way of doing things. But I'll call you later. Mom made arrangements for a phone man to come out today."

"On a Saturday?" I said in an astonished tone.

"Yup. That's Mom," Candy continued. "She has ways of getting things done."

"Candy! I'm waiting. We'll miss the phone man," Aunt Carol called.

"Come on, Betty," Mom urged. "You girls will have plenty of time to catch up later. Candy is home to stay, remember?"

"Yes, Mom," I called. "We're coming down right now."

"Sorry again about the picture," Candy

apologized as we walked out of my room.

"Forget it," I answered. "I have lots of pictures of Archie." Boy was that ever the truth!

"Did you girls have a nice chat?" Mom asked when we reached the bottom of the stairs.

"We sure did," I replied.

Mom looked at Aunt Carol. "Are you sure you won't stay for dinner?"

Aunt Carol shook her head. "Thanks Helen, but we have too much to do. I'll send out for something later." Aunt Carol nudged Candy with an elbow and winked. "We make out all right on our own, don't we, Candy Girl?"

"We sure do," Candy said.

"Isn't there anything we can do?" Dad asked.

"Well, there is one thing," Aunt Carol replied.

"What?" Dad inquired eagerly.

"You could get us our coats, Hal, unless you're holding them for ransom," teased Aunt Carol.

We all laughed. Dad went to the closet and got the coats. Everybody kissed everybody again.

"Bye, Betty. Thanks for everything,"

Candy said. "And I'm sorry again about making a mess, Aunt Helen."

"Feel free to come over and make a mess anytime," Mom answered as Aunt Carol and Candy started down the walk. They got into their rented car, started it, and drove off. We all waved.

"Carol looks good," Dad said as we shut the door. "And Candy is absolutely beautiful. You'd better watch out, Betty," he kidded. "She'll steal Archie from you and she'll break his heart."

She already broke his picture, I thought.

"How is Candy doing?" Mom asked me as Dad returned to the paper he'd been reading earlier.

"She's super," I said. "The only trouble with Candy is that she doesn't seem to have any self-confidence."

"Hmm." Mom pondered my reply. "Maybe you can help build it up," she said. "Now that Candy's moved back here, she'll need you more than ever. You and your friends have to make her feel extra welcome."

"I will, Mom," I promised. "I will." And I meant to keep that promise. Making Candy happy was very important to me.

Chapter 3

Later that night Aunt Carol phoned and told us she and Candy were, for the most part, already settled into their new house. Aunt Carol is the only person I know who could make moving day proceed like an expertly planned game of chess. All of their belongings had been promptly delivered. There were absolutely no snags to checkmate progress. It was truly astonishing the way she got things done exactly the way she wanted.

After Mom finished talking with Aunt Carol, Candy and I got on the line for a marathon conversation. We talked about everything and everyone. We shared old funny stories, like the time my doll got sucked into Mom's new vacuum cleaner and exploded the bag. We laughed the most about the time we both got into Mom's makeup to make ourselves look glamorous—and ended up looking like painted circus clowns. When I finally got off the phone I had a sore ear and an extra special feeling inside for my cousin. I would do everything I could to make her happy and popular. My friends would like her. They had to. I wouldn't let them not like her.

Early the next day my folks and I went over to Aunt Carol's to help out. Actually, Candy and I weren't much help. We unpacked crates while Dad got stuck with most of the heavy labor. Aunt Carol and Mom kept him busy shifting furniture around and around.

"Hey," Dad complained, "when do we get a lunch break? I'm pooped!"

"Lunch?" mused Aunt Carol.

"Yeah. You know . . . food." Dad clarified as he flopped into an easy chair and mopped his sweaty brow with a hanky.

"I forgot all about food," Aunt Carol admitted. "Candy and I sent out for dinner last night. We don't have a thing to eat in the house."

Gee, I thought, Aunt Carol isn't perfect after all.

"Great," Dad said, grumbling good-naturedly. "They don't even feed the slaves around here."

"I guess I'd better do some quick shopping," Aunt Carol said, reaching for her purse. "I don't want to have to deal with a rebellion."

"There's a good market right around the corner," Mom told Aunt Carol. "And they're open twenty-four hours a day, every day."

"Good," Aunt Carol replied. "I guess I'd better stop and feed the troops . . . or else."

"Say," I interrupted. "I have a suggestion. Candy and I can shop for the groceries. We can even walk there. It's beautiful out, and we won't be buying much."

"Great idea, Betty," Mom said from behind a crate filled with china.

Aunt Carol looked grateful. She handed Candy money for the groceries. "Just get enough to tide us over," Aunt Carol told her. "We can do our regular marketing later in the week."

"Right, Mom," said Candy as we got our coats and went out the front door.

We spent the walk talking about Riverdale High School. Candy had a million questions. She was really excited about starting school.

"This is it," I said when we arrived at

22

the market. "Welcome to your typical small-town grocery store."

Candy chuckled. "Okay, tour guide," Candy said. "Lead me to the gourmet points of interest, like the junk food aisle. I'll push the cart."

"Follow me," I invited, starting down the fruit and vegetable aisle.

Thumpa-thumpa-thumpa. "What's that noise?" I asked Candy.

"It's the cart," Candy told me. "The wheels are all wobbly. I guess I picked a broken one. But it's okay."

I nodded in agreement, then checked the fresh fruit on display. "The oranges look good," I said.

Candy came over to see. She pulled one out from the bottom.

"Look out!" I yelled. Plunk! Plunk! Plunk! Oranges began to tumble out one by one. Suddenly an entire avalanche of oranges spilled over the edge and dropped onto the floor. Oranges were everywhere.

"Quick, let's pick them up before somebody comes," Candy cried.

"Right," I replied, getting down on my hands and knees to collect the fallen fruit. Oranges had rolled in every direction. Luckily, the market was practically deserted at that hour and no one saw us

hunting under racks and counters like two dopey dorks.

"One went under here," I said as I got down on the floor and reached under a display. Just then a cart turned the corner.

"A polite hello is enough to greet me," someone said. "You don't have to get down on your hands and knees whenever you see me."

I looked up. It was Reggie Mantle, the Riverdale High class clown, who had an ego the size of a brontosaurus.

"Very funny, Reggie," I said, getting to my feet. I dusted off my knees. "I had to get this orange." I held up the fruit. Luckily, it wasn't damaged.

"Sure," he cracked snidely. "But right now *that* piece of fruit isn't the apple of my eye. *She* is!" He pointed at Candy, who was restacking the oranges. Reggie grinned from ear to ear and smoothed his slick black hair with his hand. "I'm sure glad Mom sent me out for milk," Reggie said. "*Orange* you going to introduce me to your friend? Ha, ha."

"She's my cousin," I explained as I led Reggie over to Candy. Candy turned toward us and smiled. Reggie's grin was so wide I thought it would crack his face.

"Reggie Mantle, allow me to present my

cousin, Candy Collins," I said. "Candy lived in Riverdale years ago. She and her mom just moved back here."

"How do you do?" Candy said sweetly.

"I'm doing better, now that I've met you," replied Reggie. He bowed, then took her hand in his and kissed it. Yuk! Reggie's antics really turned my stomach. But Candy seemed to like it. She didn't know Reggie well enough yet to realize what a phony he could sometimes be.

"Ooh, how charming," said Candy, leaning back against the fruit counter.

Plunk! Plunk! Plunk! Plunk!

"Oh no! Not the oranges again," I groaned as fruit began to fall once more.

"Let me help you," Reggie offered.

"It's okay, I'll do it," Candy said. They bent forward at the same time. *Bonk!* Their heads knocked together with a resounding noise.

"Ouch!" cried Reggie, in pain. "You broke my head!"

"S-sorry," Candy apologized.

"It's okay—I think," Reggie replied, rubbing his forehead. "What's a little concussion between friends?"

I ignored Reggie's wisecrack. "Let's get the fruit back where it belongs before the manager shows up," I suggested. And we did just that. Quickly, we collected and restacked every single orange.

"Thanks for your help, Reggie," Candy said. She put her hands on our cart and prepared to shove off. "I'll look forward to seeing you in school tomorrow."

"Ah, right! It sure was nice bumping into you," Reggie answered as he rubbed the lump swelling on his forehead.

"See ya, Reg," I said as Candy pushed our cart forward. Thumpa-thumpa-thumpa.

"Yeow!" Reggie shouted. He lifted his right foot and started to hop.

"What's wrong now?" I asked, halting in my tracks.

"Your cousin just ran over my toes," Reggie bellowed as he bounced up and down on one leg.

"Oh, Reggie, I'm so sorry," Candy apologized. She started toward him. "Here, let me help you."

"No! No thanks." Reggie backed away from Candy in fear. He snatched the jug of milk from his cart. "Don't come near me. Stay away. I want to get out of here alive." Off he bounced toward the check-out counter as if a pack of wolves were snapping at his heels.

"Gee, I hope I didn't make a bad impression," Candy said.

"Impression? It was more like a dent . . . in his foot," I joked. We both burst out laughing.

"Seriously, though," said Candy. "I hope Reggie isn't mad at me."

"Don't worry about Reggie," I advised. "When you get to know him, you'll learn to ignore him like everyone else does. He's a joker, a con artist, and a troublemaker. But if you overlook those qualities, he's not half bad."

"I think he's kind of cute," confessed Candy. "Do you think he liked me?"

"I think he found you different from anyone he's ever met before," I assured her.

"Good! In fact . . . awesome!" said Candy as she shoved the cart down the aisle. Thumpa-thumpa-thumpa!

Chapter 4

Monday morning I had arranged to meet Candy near the student bulletin board outside the main office. We didn't go to school together that first day because Candy had to arrive an hour early to finish her registration and to go over her schedule with the guidance counselor.

I checked my wristwatch for the third time. I was anxious to introduce Candy to my friends before class.

"Excuse me, Vetty," someone said. I turned to see the school janitor, Mr. Svenson, who spoke with a thick Swedish accent. He was holding a mop and a bucket of water. "I gott to mop up the hall," he explained.

"Sure, Mr. Svenson," I replied, moving out of his way to the far end of the bulletin board. Mr. Svenson placed the bucket of sudsy water on the floor near the office and began to mop.

"Hi, Betty. What are you waiting for?" Midge Klump asked as she walked up with Veronica Lodge.

"Hi, Midge! Hi, Ron!" I said, greeting my friends with a big smile. My smile faltered a little when I saw what Veronica was wearing. Ronnie had on an expensive, utterly gorgeous suit. It was so dazzling it made the dress I was wearing look like a cheap sale item. (Actually, I did get it on sale!) I sighed. Being friends—and rivals—with the wealthiest girl in town sometimes presented problems. "I like your outfit," I said to Ron. "Is it new?"

"This old thing, new?" remarked Ron. "Hardly! I'm about ready to donate it to charity." She looked at me with a smug expression on her face. "Well, are you coming to homeroom or not?" Veronica asked impatiently as I stood there, dumbfounded by her expensive attire.

"Yes. I mean no," I answered. "I have to wait for my cousin Candy. She's in the office."

"Your cousin finally arrived?" said Midge. "How nice! I can't wait to meet her. What's she like?"

"Yes," added Veronica coolly. "What is

she like? Homely, I hope. Competition for the boys around here is tough enough already." After a moment's hesitation, she added, "Not that I can't handle it."

"Well?" urged Midge. "Are you going to tell us what Candy is like, or not?"

"Candy is nice," I said, searching for the right description. "And she's very attractive."

"She's a total babe," Reggie Mantle confirmed, walking up with Archie Andrews and Jughead Jones. Jughead was munching on a donut. He was Riverdale's own bottomless pit. Snacking wasn't a hobby to Jughead, it was a vocation. He just loved to eat.

"Candy is dandy," Reggie continued, "but she's dangerous."

I winced. I wondered what Reggie was going to say next.

"Is she a karate expert or something?" Archie asked.

"Nope," Reggie replied, shaking his head. "She's more lethal than that."

"Reggie Mantle!" I snapped angrily. I waved a fist in front of his nose in a warning fashion. "If you make one nasty remark about my cousin, I'll rearrange your face."

Quickly, Reggie raised his hands in surrender. "Hey! I'm not being nasty. I'm just telling the truth," he swore.

Just then, as if on cue, the office door opened. Out stepped Candy. She didn't see me. She was dressed in a tight leather mini and a white sweater. Her long, blonde hair was styled perfectly.

"Wow," sighed Archie.

"Hmph!" grunted Veronica, twisting up her lips in an expression of disdain.

"What could be dangerous about her?" Jughead asked as he started on a candy bar he'd taken out of his pocket. "She's just an ordinary girl."

"She looks dangerous to me," Ronnie muttered.

"Candy!" I called, waving my arm. "Over here!"

"Hi, Betty!" yelled Candy. She rushed across the hall without noticing Mr. Svenson or his bucket.

"Look out!" cried Mr. Svenson. Candy kicked the bucket over and soapy water spilled all over the hall.

"What in the world is going on out here?" yelled Mr. Weatherbee, the school principal, from his office. He rushed into the hall. "Yeow!" His feet hit the water and slipped out from under him, and Mr. Weatherbee ended up on the seat of his

pants in the middle of a soapy puddle. "Svenson!" he hollered. His angry voice echoed down the hall. "Who? What? How?" he sputtered.

"I told you she was dangerous to be around," whispered Reggie out of the side of his mouth.

"So I see," Veronica replied softly. Archie and Jughead raced over to help the Bee (which is our nickname for Mr. Weatherbee). As Archie bent over to assist Mr. Weatherbee, he stepped on a wet spot and slipped to the floor himself. Luckily, the spot he landed on was dry.

"Archie Andrews!" grumbled Mr. Weatherbee, glaring at Archie. "I should have guessed it was you."

"B-b-but it wasn't me, sir," stammered Archie. "I'm innocent."

"Then who did it?" Mr. Weatherbee demanded as he and Archie got to their feet.

Archie pointed at Candy. "But it was just an accident, sir," he explained. "She accidentally kicked over the bucket of water."

Mr. Weatherbee peered at Candy. "Do I know you?" he asked sternly.

Candy shook her head. She was too terrified to speak. It was time for me to rush to her rescue.

"She's new here, sir," I said. "She's my cousin, Candy Collins. Today is her first day." I turned toward Candy. "Candy, this is Mr. Weatherbee, our school principal." Candy's eyes opened wide in shock.

Mr. Weatherbee looked at me. Then he looked back at Candy. "Hmm," he mumbled thoughtfully, stroking his chin. "I guess it could've happened to anyone."

Reggie coughed as if to dispute that comment. A glance from the Bee silenced him.

Mr. Weatherbee continued. "Betty is one of our finest students," he told Candy. "I hope you'll take after her and we'll have no more of these little accidents, Miss Collins."

Candy gulped and nodded. She was still too scared to speak.

Mr. Weatherbee turned away. "Now, if you'll excuse me, I have to change this wet suit."

We all chuckled as Mr. Weatherbee walked off, stiff-legged. "Dat vas berry funny," said Mr. Svenson. He righted the overturned bucket and started to mop up the water.

"I'm just glad Mr. Weatherbee wasn't hurt," Candy said, finally finding her voice.

"That's because he's well padded," kidded Reggie. "Especially the part he fell on." No one laughed.

Candy turned to Archie. "So you're Archie Andrews," she said. "I think we met a long time ago, when we were little."

"I don't remember," Archie admitted. "And I can't imagine I'd forget someone as pretty as you."

I heard Veronica grunt behind us. Candy blushed a rosy red.

"I'm sorry I almost got you in trouble, Archie," Candy apologized.

"Don't worry about that," Archie replied.

"Yeah," teased Jughead. "Most of the time when things go wrong around here, it *is* Archie's fault. He automatically gets blamed for everything." Archie gave Jug a dirty look. Jug just shrugged and started to unwrap another candy bar.

"Candy," I said to my cousin, "I'd like you to meet my friends." I introduced her to everyone. Midge was especially warm and friendly in her greetings to Candy. Veronica was nice, but sounded a little jealous.

"I'm pleased to meet all of you," Candy said. "I hope we can all become very good friends."

"I'm sure we will," Midge replied.

"Yeah," Reggie whispered to Veronica behind Candy's back. "Just make sure your medical insurance is paid up." Luckily, Candy didn't hear Reggie's wise remark.

Just then the bell rang. "Get going," Mr. Svenson said. "Dat is da bell. Time for homeroom."

I checked Candy's schedule. Just as I'd expected, she was in the same homeroom as Veronica, Midge, and I, and in all of our classes.

"See you later, girls," Archie said as he and the guys headed for their own homerooms.

"Stick with us, Candy," said Midge, leading the way. "You'll soon learn your way around here. Riverdale is a small school."

"Just watch out for buckets," Veronica joked.

"Yeah, right," said Candy. She pretended Ronnie's comment hadn't hurt her. I knew it had. There was no way I could smooth it over, so I just kept silent. But it hurt me, too.

Chapter 5

As we walked down the hall, we talked universal school gossip. We discussed who was going out with whom, who was breaking up with whom, and who was wearing what. I couldn't help mentioning again how impressed I was with Veronica's suit.

"It's just a little something I picked up in Europe last year," Veronica commented casually, as if every girl in Riverdale could afford to do her shopping abroad.

"Say," Midge began as we neared our homeroom, "whose turn is it to be homework hound?"

"Homework hound? What's that?" asked Candy.

"It's simple," I began. "Since all of us are in the same classes, one person copies down the day's homework assignments in every class. Then we all meet at Pop

Tate's, the corner soda shop, and copy the assignments from the homework hound, at our leisure. It makes things a lot easier during the school day."

"It sure does," Midge agreed. "Now who's today's hound?"

"I'll do it," Candy volunteered.

We stopped outside homeroom. I looked at my cousin. "I don't know, Candy," I said. "After all, it is your first day."

"Oh, let her do it," Veronica urged. "It's not like it's complicated or anything. All she has to do is write down the homework."

"Don't worry, Betty," Candy said to me. "I won't mess up."

"It's not that—" I began.

"Then that settles it," Midge stated as she entered Miss Grundy's homeroom. "Candy is the homework hound for today." Veronica smiled at us and followed Midge in.

The bell rang. Candy sat down in an empty seat two desks in front of me. It was the only open seat in the room.

"Students," Miss Grundy called. "Settle down. I have some announcements to make." When the class was quiet, Miss Grundy read the announcements about clubs, sports, and other school activities— the usual boring stuff. After that, we stood for the salute to the flag and the Pledge of Allegiance. When we were seated again, Miss Grundy spoke.

"Class," she began, "I'd like to introduce a brand-new student. Her name is Candace Collins. Today is her first day at Riverdale High. I hope you'll all welcome her to our school. Please stand, Candace."

Shyly, Candy got to her feet. Some of the more rowdy boys whistled and made wolf calls. Miss Grundy quickly got them to stop. Candy blushed and eased back into her seat.

"Candace," continued Miss Grundy, "I'm sure you'll be very happy here at Riverdale High. I'll see you later in my literature class." Miss Grundy was one of the best teachers at Riverdale High. She was also a successful, liberated single woman who always spoke her mind. I liked her a lot.

The bell rang.

"Homeroom is dismissed," Miss Grundy announced.

I got up and joined Candy. Together, we started to file out behind the rest of the class. As we passed Miss Grundy, she spoke to Candy.

"I hear that you're Betty's cousin," Miss Grundy told her. "I'm pleased that you'll be in my class. I hope your first day here in school will be a happy one."

"Thank you, Miss Grundy," Candy said. "I'm sure I'm going to like it here."

We both smiled at Miss Grundy and went out to join Veronica and Midge, who were waiting for us in the hall.

"This is going to be an exciting day," Candy said as we headed for our first class.

"I'm sure it will be," I said to my cousin.

Unfortunately for Candy, her first day at school was a little *too* exciting. Things went awry right after first period. On the way to second-period class, Candy stopped in the girls' room while I continued on. Since the class was just down the hall from the lavatory, I figured nothing could go wrong. But it did! Somehow Candy took a wrong turn and got lost. She finally wandered into biology class ten minutes late. Luckily, Professor Flutesnoot was understanding. Veronica thought the whole thing was a riot, but I was just embarrassed for Candy.

I didn't think it was funny, either, when Candy made the mistake of going in the "out" door of the cafeteria lunch line—another simple mistake that could have happened to anyone. When she bumped into Jughead and sent his trayful of food flying every which way, almost the whole cafeteria broke into laughter. But I didn't see anything hilarious about spaghetti sailing through the air and splattering all over the floor. And I know Jughead didn't laugh. Candy didn't laugh. Mr. Svenson didn't laugh when he was called in to clean up the mess. Jughead's smile returned quickly, though, when Candy bought him another lunch—and an extra dessert.

But that wasn't the end of Candy's troubles. In gym, our last class of the day, Candy's locker got stuck, and she couldn't get the sneakers she'd put in there earlier that morning. Candy had to go to class wearing just socks and made a spectacle of herself, slipping all over the floor during volleyball. Her team lost three games in a row. We were both glad when the class ended.

"What a day!" sighed Candy after the final bell rang.

"First days are always rough," I comforted her. "It'll get better once you get into the flow of things."

"With my luck, I'll end up as a clog in the flow," joked Candy. I chuckled—but I wasn't so sure my cousin was kidding.

"A soda at Pop Tate's will make you feel

better," I said as we walked out of the building. "Midge and Veronica are probably there already."

I was right. Midge called out to us as we walked through the door of the soda shop. "Well, it's about time," she said.

"What did you do, get lost?" Veronica asked sarcastically.

Reggie chuckled. He must have heard that Candy had gotten lost on the way to biology.

"It was my fault," I said curtly. "I forgot a book and we had to go back for it." I didn't want to embarrass my cousin further by having everyone hear about the gym locker mishap.

Candy looked at me and smiled. We sat down in the booth next to Midge and Veronica.

"Speaking of books," Midge began. She looked at Candy. "You might as well give us the bad news right now, homework hound."

Candy started to sift through her notebook papers. "I have it all written down right here," Candy said.

"First things first," I interrupted as Pop Tate, the owner of the soda shop, came over to take our order. I introduced my cousin to Pop.

"New business is always welcome," Pop said jovially. "What will it be, girls?"

"Two strawberry milkshakes," I answered. "And make them double thick. We've had a really rough day."

"That's for sure," Candy agreed, continuing to search through her notebook.

Archie and Jughead soon arrived at Pop's and came over to the table. Archie bumped into a chair and almost knocked it over as he approached us. "Hi, guys," I greeted them.

"Oh," exclaimed Candy. "Here it is." She pulled a paper out. Midge, Veronica, and I took out paper and prepared to write down our homework assignments for the night.

"For history, read pages thirty to fifty-five," Candy said, "and answer questions one to ten at the end of the chapter." Candy paused before going on. "For algebra II, do problems twelve to twenty on page thirty-five."

"Wait a minute," Archie butted in. Archie was also in our algebra class. "I think that's wrong."

"You must be mistaken," Candy protested. "I'm sure this is right."

Archie shook his head. "I went in for extra algebra help after class," he explained. "Those aren't the homework problems we did." He took out his algebra book and clumsily dropped it on the floor. "Whoops!" he said as he bent over to pick it up. Quickly, he opened the book. "I was right. Tonight's homework is problems twelve to thirty-five on page twenty."

"And that history homework is wrong, too," Reggie added as he flipped through his history book. Reg was in that class with us. "The assignment is to read pages thirty to forty-five and answer questions one, three, five, and ten at the end of the chapter."

Candy froze. It was very quiet. Midge looked at Veronica. Veronica glared at Candy and shook her head. Midge looked at me.

"We could have done all the wrong homework assignments because of her," groaned Midge. "Luckily, the guys stopped her when they did."

"She goofs everything up," snapped Veronica. "That cousin of yours is really something, Betty Cooper."

"Don't talk about my cousin like that, Veronica Lodge, or you'll have to spend part of your father's fortune on a good nose job." I couldn't believe she would say those things right in front of Candy.

Tears welled up in Candy's eyes. She quietly collected her books and papers. "Veronica is right," she admitted. "They have a right to be mad at me. I am a goof-up."

"B-but you're a beautiful goof-up," said Archie, trying to make a joke to smooth things over. "That's one better than me."

"Excuse me," Candy said. Before I could stop her, she slipped out of the booth and ran out the door, crying.

Veronica gulped. "I didn't mean to hurt her feelings," Veronica apologized. "I guess I just didn't think."

"I'm sorry, too," said Midge. "I over-reacted."

"Yeah," echoed Reggie. "Candy can't help it if she goofs everything up. It just comes naturally to her."

I got up. I was too angry to say anything. Pop Tate came over with our shakes. I gave him the money we owed him and picked up my books.

"Aren't you going to drink them?" Pop asked.

"No," I replied. "I'm particular who I drink with."

"Don't be mad, Betty," said Archie. "They didn't mean to hurt Candy's feelings."

"I know," I said. "It's just that Candy is very special to me. I want everything to go right for her."

"Things will sort themselves out," Archie said. "It'll just take time."

"Right," echoed Jughead. "It's just like cooking. Things have to simmer a bit before they're done."

"Great," I said. "Now I better try to simmer down my poor cousin." I walked away from the booth and went out the door.

Chapter 6

All the way to Candy's house I kept trying to think of what I could say to her. How could I make her feel better about herself? I honestly didn't know. I decided to play it by ear. I rang the bell and waited. Nobody answered. I rang again and again. I knew Candy was in there and needed me. Finally, she peeked out the window and then reluctantly opened the door. Her eyes were red. She'd been crying.

"I didn't think you were going to let me in," I said, walking into the living room. Candy closed the door behind me.

"I don't feel like talking," Candy explained. "I want to be alone."

I dropped my books on the sofa and took off my coat. "I think we need to talk," I said firmly as I flopped on the couch. "We've always been as close as sisters. Sisters stick together, no matter what. So what's the problem, Sis?"

A trace of a smile spread across Candy's face. She sat down in a chair opposite me. "You know what the trouble is," Candy began. "And after only one day in school, so does everyone else. Candy Collins is a klutz and a goof-up. Veronica is right."

"Veronica Lodge talks too much," I replied.

"No. She's right about me, and you and I both know it," Candy continued. "At my old school, my nickname was Klutzy Candy. Everyone avoided me like I had the plague."

Candy sighed. "I thought things would be different here. I thought I could make a fresh start. But I'm still stupid old Klutzy Candy!"

I leaned forward. "That's a bunch of baloney!" I said sternly. "The only thing wrong with you is that you lack self-confidence. You're so worried about making a good impression that you get all jittery and mess up."

Candy stared at me as if she wanted to believe what I'd said.

"You can change if you want to. You'll just have to work hard at it," I said encouragingly.

Slowly, Candy shook her head. "I wish that was true," Candy muttered. "I've tried in the past and it never worked. How can a mother who never makes any mistakes have a daughter who makes nothing but mistakes?" Candy sniffed. She looked like she was going to start crying again.

"Everyone makes mistakes," I corrected. "Even your mom."

"The only mistakes my mom ever made were getting married and having me," Candy lamented. "There's not a single thing I can do right."

"Baloney!" I said. "You just haven't found your niche. I'll bet there's something you're really good at. We just haven't found it yet. And I'm going to help you look."

Candy threw her arms around me and hugged me tightly. "Oh, Betty!" she cried. "You're the best cousin anyone ever had."

"*You're* the best cousin anyone ever had," I fired back. "Now I've got to get home. Stop worrying about what happened today, and get ready to knock Riverdale High dead tomorrow." I headed for the door. "I'll call you later tonight."

"Great," Candy said. She was smiling.

"Then you can give me the right homework to do."

I laughed and went out the door.

When I got home Mom was in the kitchen preparing dinner. "Hi, Mom! Need any help?" I asked as I deposited my books on the kitchen counter.

"Not just now, dear," Mom answered. "How was Candy's first day at Riverdale High?"

I took off my coat and sat down at the table. I put my elbows on the table and propped my chin in my hands. "Don't ask. It was a total disaster," I replied.

Mom turned away from the stove. "What happened?" she asked, concerned.

I spilled the beans. I told Mom everything, starting with the water bucket and ending with the wrong homework assignments. Mom punctuated my tale of woe with chuckles here and there, and by the time I finished, she was laughing hysterically.

"Candy sure takes after her mother," Mom said.

"What?" I exclaimed. I was totally puzzled. "Run that by me again."

"Candy is just like her mother was in high school," Mom said.

"You mean Aunt Carol?" I said, shocked. "My Aunt Carol was a klutz, too?"

Mom caught her breath. She'd laughed so hard there were tears in her eyes. "In those days we didn't use words like geek, klutz, or nerd," Mom explained. "But that's what Aunt Carol was. Everyone used to say she had ten thumbs and two left feet. Carol broke anything that wasn't nailed down."

I was utterly flabbergasted. Could it be true? My perfect Aunt Carol had once been a klutz just like my cousin Candy was now? Go figure! "Mom, are you kidding me?" I asked, looking for some additional information.

"I swear it's the truth," Mom vowed, holding up her right hand. "Your perfect aunt used to be called Clumsy Carol."

"But what happened to her?" I sputtered. "How did she change so much?"

"She grew out of her clumsiness," Mom replied. "Candy will grow out of it, too. You'll see."

I thought for a minute. Candy believed her mom was perfect. If she could only hear what I just heard, it might help her out. "Mom," I said, "would you tell Candy what you just told me about Aunt Carol?"

Mom sat down across from me. "I don't think it's my place to tell Candy her mother's history," she said. "And I don't think it's your job either, Betty Cooper."

"But Mom," I argued, "Candy is really down on herself. If she knew her mom once had the same problems, it might make her feel better."

Mom nodded. "I agree. But I think the information should come from Aunt Carol herself. I don't want to interfere."

I exhaled loudly. I guessed Mom was right, but it was hard to accept.

Mom put her hand on my arm. "Don't worry," she said. "Everything will work out. How about if I invite Candy and Aunt Carol to dinner on Friday? Maybe in the course of normal conversation all of this will come to light."

I grinned. "Mom, you're one sly little devil."

Mom grinned back. "Like mother, like daughter," she said, winking across the table at me.

Chapter 7

I was sure glad when that first week of school was over! Anything that could have gone wrong did! On Tuesday, Candy saw a loose string hanging from Veronica's sweater. She tried to be helpful and pull it off and ended up ruining a very expensive cashmere top. Veronica was furious but, for my sake, she controlled her temper.

On Wednesday, Candy paired up with Midge in home economics class. Their assignment was to bake a cake. Midge's foolproof recipe had never failed to get an A+ before. Of course, that was before Midge had a partner like my cousin Candy. Candy made a slight mistake. She accidentally substituted black pepper for cinnamon. When Miss Martin, the home ec teacher, sampled the cake, she almost passed out. Midge and Candy were lucky to have gotten a D. To Midge's credit, she didn't lose her temper either.

On Thursday I had high hopes for Candy. It was in gym class, and we were playing field hockey outside. The boys were playing touch football in the field next to us. Our field hockey game was so good, some of the boys, including Archie, watched from the sidelines. Candy looked great—she was very athletic.

With the score tied three-all, Candy made a super steal and started to move in for a goal shot. She faked out two defenders and had an open net. It looked like she'd win the game for sure. Then Candy fired a wicked shot that ricocheted off the net's pole and ended up hitting Archie on the knee. He screamed like a banshee when the ball hit him.

For a few minutes, everyone was really concerned. After all, Archie is the starting quarterback on the football team, and the season opener wasn't far off. Luckily, Archie ended up with just a bruise and another apology from Candy.

Then came Friday. Just forget about Friday! I won't even mention the lab frogs getting loose in science class or the bubble-gum bubble that Candy burst in my hair (I didn't lose *too* much) or the fountain pen that exploded on the radiator in literature class. Like I said, it was quite a first week for Candy.

What made things even worse was watching how depressed Candy got as the week wore on. I know if I could have told her about Aunt Carol's past, it would have helped a lot. But I'd promised Mom I would keep silent, and I did. Still, I couldn't wait for Friday to arrive so Mom and I could coax Aunt Carol into talking about her high school mishaps. And at long last that moment came.

"What a delicious meal," Aunt Carol complimented Mom as we dined on the main course. "You always were the best cook in the family, Helen."

"Thanks, Carol," Mom replied. She looked at Candy. "Is everything okay?" she asked.

"It's great," said Candy. Then she turned to me and whispered, "So far, so good. I haven't spilled anything yet."

"Whispering at the dinner table isn't polite," Aunt Carol reprimanded Candy.

"Don't be so stuffy, Carol," Dad joked. "After all, it's just family here."

"That's true, Hal," Aunt Carol replied coolly. "But it's best not to get into rude habits, even with family."

Dad shrugged and accepted the rebuff without further comment, and returned to the business of emptying his plate.

"Knowing Betty, they were probably whispering about boys," Mom said. "You know how high school girls are, Carol. Remember when we were in high school?"

There was a sudden lull in the conversation. I shifted my gaze to Aunt Carol. "I don't remember whispering at the dinner table," Aunt Carol answered. Then she continued to eat. It was obvious she wasn't going to elaborate.

"Gee, Aunt Carol," I blurted out, "what were you and Mom like in high school?"

Aunt Carol slowly placed her fork on the table. She smiled. "All the boys chased after your mom, Betty," she answered. "She was the beautiful one."

"She still is beautiful," Dad chimed in.

"Thanks, Hal," said Mom. "And thank you, too, Carol. But you weren't exactly an ugly duckling. Lots of boys liked you, too. You were very popular."

Aunt Carol blushed. "Let's not rehash the old days," she said, trying to change the subject. "It's so boring."

"I'm not bored, Mom," protested Candy. "I'd like to know what you were like when you were my age. You've never told me anything about your teenage days."

Aunt Carol looked flustered. Her cheeks flushed. Then she regained her composure. "I was exactly the same person I am today, except younger," she answered. "Now let's talk about you two girls. Did Betty introduce you to any interesting boys, Candy?"

Candy glanced at me sideways. "Y-yes. I met a few boys."

"Did you meet Archie Andrews?" quizzed Dad. "That Archie is quite a character. He's like a teenage accident looking for a place to happen." Dad chuckled. He didn't realize his offhand comments about Archie were just as true for Candy.

I looked at my cousin. I felt bad for her. And I felt angry with my aunt. Aunt Carol never let her defenses down, not even for an instant. She enjoyed being perfect so much that she didn't want anyone, including her own daughter, to suspect she'd ever been anything less than perfect.

I sneaked a peek at my mom. Mom must have read my mind. She raised her eyebrows and shrugged as if to say, That's that!

"Candy hasn't talked much about school at home this week," Aunt Carol continued. "How's everything going?"

"It's going great!" I broke in. "All the boys are chasing after Candy. Every girl in school is jealous of her."

A surprised look came over Aunt Carol's face. "R-really?" she sputtered. "That's wonderful!"

"Yup," I continued. "Candy is really a hit. In fact, she and I are double-dating next Saturday night."

"Hey! That's nice," Dad complimented. He didn't realize that I was making things up as I went along.

"Who are you two going out with?" Aunt Carol asked Candy.

Candy looked baffled. She turned to me. "Ah, who are we going out with?" she mumbled.

"See that?" I said. "So many boys have asked her out already, she can't even remember who we're dating." I looked at Candy. "It's Reggie Mantle and Archie Andrews," I prompted. "Remember?"

"Oh right! Reggie and Archie," Candy said, playing along.

"I used to bounce these girls on my knees. Now they're double-dating. Life sure goes fast," groaned Dad.

"This dinner sure went fast," Mom said. "It's time for dessert already."

"I'll get it," I offered.

"I'll help," Candy added. We quickly cleared the table and carted the dishes into the kitchen.

"Thanks for trying to make me look good in front of my mom," Candy said when we were alone. "But what's going to happen next Saturday when she finds me sitting home instead of going out?"

"She won't," I assured my cousin. "Next Saturday you and I really *are* going on a double date with Reggie and Archie."

"Oh Betty, that's wonderful," Candy cried. "How did you manage it?"

"There was nothing to manage," I said. "It was easy. The boys are dying to take us out."

Chapter 8

"I wouldn't be caught dead dating that female jinx," Reggie said when I cornered him and Archie the following week at Pop Tate's and proposed the date. "Candy is a doll, but the woman is poison. A guy could end up in traction, hanging around her."

"Give it a rest, Reg," Archie said. "Candy isn't that clumsy. Think how impressed everyone would be to see you with such a gorgeous gal."

Reggie stroked his chin thoughtfully and considered the idea.

"That's right," I said, picking up on Archie's argument. "Just think of going out to eat and to a movie with a beautiful, shapely blonde on your arm. Reggie Mantle would be the envy of every guy in town."

"Hmm . . ." Reggie grunted. His forehead furrowed in concentration. Presenting a cool-guy image was really important to Reggie. We had him interested.

"Well, Reg, what do you say?" Archie prodded. "Do you agree to the double date?"

"Okay, Carrot Crop Top," Reggie agreed, ribbing Archie about his hair. "You talked me into it. I'll go on a double date with Betty and Candy—on one condition."

"Good!" cried Archie.

"What's the condition?" I asked.

"My date is Betty," Reggie said, grinning. "Archie has to be Candy's date."

"B-b-but Betty is supposed to be my date," Archie stammered.

"That's right," I argued.

"Fine," said Reggie. "Then I don't go."

"But what about having a beautiful girl on your arm?" I said.

"I will, Sweetiekins," Reggie said. "*You'll* be on my arm. Candy will be on Archie's arm. And if Arch is lucky, she won't break it off for him." Reggie folded his arms and stared at me. "That's my final offer. Take it or leave it."

Archie took me aside. He shrugged his shoulders. "I guess he's got us where he wants us. But I don't like your going out with him."

"I don't have any choice." I sighed. "If I don't go with him, Candy doesn't go out on a double date."

"You could always take Candy out by yourself, Arch," Reggie suggested in a smart-aleck way. He'd overheard everything.

Archie looked at me again. I looked back at him. "No way," Archie said.

"No way," I repeated. I loved my cousin, but some things were asking just too much. And one of those things was letting my cousin go out on a date all alone with the guy of my dreams.

"If it's okay with Betty, then it's okay with me," Archie agreed reluctantly. "I'll take Candy on our double date."

"It's okay with me." I sighed again. "I'll be your date, Reggie."

"You won't regret it, Blondie," cackled a triumphant Reggie. "This will be the best date of your life." He grinned from ear to ear and winked at me. "Oh, and one more thing," Reg added before walking away. "Archie has to pay for everything." He laughed, and strutted off like a peacock.

"That Reggie is a slithering, slimy, scheming snake," grumbled Archie. "One of these days I'm going to . . ."

"Forget it, Archiekins," I said. "He's got us over a barrel and he knows it. I just hope Candy has a good time after all this."

"I'll see to it that she has a good time," Archie promised.

I looked at Archie enviously. At least somebody would have a good time on our double date. I sure wasn't going to, stuck with Mr. Super Ego, Reggie Mantle. Even worse, I'd have to watch another girl go out with my Archie.

Chapter 9

"How do I look?" Candy asked. We were at her house, getting ready for our big double date. Candy looked sensational. If she hadn't been my cousin I'd probably have been jealous of her. Her makeup, hair, and clothes were perfect. She had on a mini-skirt and blouse with a matching jacket.

"You're a real babe," I had to admit. "Archie is going to flip for you."

"I guess that's teen talk for beautiful," Aunt Carol said, walking up to us. "And I agree one hundred percent." She turned to look at me. "But Betty, you're no slouch either," she complimented. "That white dress is really very attractive."

"Thank you, Aunt Carol," I replied. What I had on wasn't actually new, but it was one of my favorite dresses. I'd considered wearing something ordinary because I was only going out with Reggie. But then

I thought better of it. I didn't want to turn off Archie along with Reggie. Then again, I didn't want to show up my cousin either. Choosing a dress that looked just right, but not too good, took some time. I'd settled for one of my old favorites.

"Do you have to meet the boys, Mom?" Candy asked her mother as we waited impatiently for them to arrive. "It'll look so juvenile. It'll seem like you're checking them out before letting me go out with them."

"That's exactly what I am doing," Aunt Carol admitted. "We've just moved here. Though I trust Betty's judgment, I want to know who you'll be with and where you're going."

Candy fidgeted on the sofa. "Your mom is right," I said to Candy. "My mom makes me introduce everyone I go out with, too. Don't worry. Archie and Reggie are used to the third degree." We all laughed.

Candy leaned close to me. "I still don't understand why Archie is taking me out instead of you," she whispered. "He's your boyfriend, isn't he?"

"Not really," I said. "I wish he were. He dates Veronica Lodge and lots of other girls, too. Archie likes to play the field. But if I do have to share Archie, you're the person I'd most like to share him with."

Candy smiled. Just then we heard a car pull into the driveway. Candy jumped to her feet. In her excitement she almost knocked a lamp off the end table. I steadied it just in time.

"Boy, am I nervous," she announced, reaching for her coat.

"Relax, Cousin," I said as I picked up my own coat. "This is going to be the first of many dates for you here in Riverdale."

The bell rang. All three of us went to answer the door. "Ready, ladies?" Aunt Carol asked as the doorbell sounded a second time. Candy and I grinned and nodded. Aunt Carol put her hand on the doorknob, turned it, and slowly pulled open the door.

"Good evening, Ms. Collins," Archie greeted. "I'm Archie Andrews." He then turned to Reggie, standing beside him on the stoop. "This is Reggie Mantle. Are Candy and Betty ready?"

"We sure are," I said.

"Come in, boys," Aunt Carol invited. "I'm delighted to meet such charming and polite young men."

"Wow," said Reggie after he and Archie stepped in. "You girls look great!"

"You sure do," Archie agreed.

Candy blushed. "Thank you," she said.

"Well, what are we waiting for?" I said. "We don't want to be late for the movie."

"Right," Archie said, offering his arm to Candy. "Bye, Ms. Collins. It was nice meeting you."

"Bye," echoed Reggie as he and I headed for the door.

"Good-bye," called Aunt Carol. "Be careful and have a good time."

"Bye, Mom," Candy called back.

We walked to the driveway where Archie's bright red jalopy was parked. Reggie rolled his eyes and slapped the jalopy's side.

"Why couldn't we have taken my car instead of this wreck on wheels?" he complained as we climbed in.

"Hey, watch what you say about Ol' Betsy!" Archie warned Reggie. "She's sensitive."

"I think Ol' Betsy is very nice," Candy said.

"Thank you," answered Archie. He turned the ignition key. Ol' Betsy's engine sputtered, rumbled, and hissed. Then it backfired a few times. Ka-pow! Ka-pow!

"Listen to that motor purr," said Archie as we backed out and then headed for the movie theater.

"Lucky the movie house isn't far," Reggie wisecracked.

"Don't pay any attention to him, Ol' girl," Archie said, patting the dashboard of his car.

We rumbled, bumped, and backfired our way to the movie theater. During the drive we talked about school. I spent most of my time pushing Reggie's arm off my shoulders.

"Here we are," Archie finally announced, to my relief. "Gee, it sure is crowded. The lot is full—I'll have to park in the street."

We found a spot about a block from the theater. "I hate having to pay to park," Archie complained, reaching into his pocket for some change for the meter.

"The treat's on me," offered Candy. "I'll get the meter."

"Thanks," said Archie. He got out of the car and started around the other side to open Candy's door. "Oh no!" he yelled when he passed the front of Ol' Betsy. He stopped and crouched down.

"What is it?" Candy asked. We all got out to take a look.

"My radiator is leaking again," moaned Archie.

"Your brain is leaking," Reggie

snapped. "It's only a tiny leak. Worry about it later. Let's get to the movie."

"Okay! Okay!" said Archie.

Off we went down the street. "I think your car is totally radical," Candy said to Archie as we strolled down the sidewalk.

"It's a total piece of junk," muttered Reggie, who never had anything good to say about anything.

"What movie are we going to see?" I asked, trying to change the subject.

"It's a horror flick," Archie replied. "I hope horror flicks don't scare you," he said to Candy.

"They do, but I love them," Candy replied, snuggling close to Archie.

I bit my lip. Watching Candy with Archie wasn't as easy as I thought it would be. I especially didn't like the way Archie was staring deep into her eyes and grinning like a lovesick puppy. He was enjoying his date a little too much.

"Hey, Betty, are you paying any attention at all to what I'm saying?" asked Reggie.

"Huh? What?" I sputtered.

"I've been talking to you for five minutes and all you do is stare at Archie and Candy," Reggie said.

"Sorry, Reg," I apologized. "I'll try not to ignore you so much once we're inside the movie."

"Thanks, I think," said Reggie as we followed Candy and Archie up to the ticket booth.

Once inside, the guys stopped at the snack counter for a supply of soda and popcorn. I waited with Candy.

"I'm having a good time already," Candy confided as Archie paid for the snacks. "Not one thing has gone wrong. I feel like a new person."

"Maybe you are," I encouraged her.

The four of us entered the theater. We found good seats about halfway up the aisle on the right side. Candy and I sat between Archie and Reggie. We were no sooner seated than the lights dimmed and the movie started.

The movie was really scary, the kind where the audience begins to shriek almost immediately. I sat riveted in my chair. Several times I had to look away. Candy did, too.

"Popcorn?" offered Reggie. He seemed to be totally unaffected by the blood and gore on the screen. In fact, I think he kind of liked it.

"N-n-no th-thank you," I mumbled.

Just then a really gross scene came on. "*Eek!*" I yelled, turning away.

"*Eek!*" Candy screamed. I felt her jerk toward Archie.

"*Yeow!*" Archie bellowed. He jumped to his feet and sent a bucket of popcorn sailing skyward. Pieces of popcorn showered everyone in our vicinity.

"Sit down, Arch!" griped Reggie. "What are you, chicken?"

"No," sputtered Archie. "I'm cold and wet. Candy just dumped a container of icy soda into my lap."

"Oh, no," Candy lamented.

"Sit down," someone a few rows behind us hollered.

"Down in front," another person complained.

"We'd better go out into the lobby," I suggested.

"Sure, fine," grumbled Reggie. "Right at the best part of the movie. That girl's going to get her head chopped off any minute, and I'm going to miss it."

"Move it, Mantle," I ordered. I guess Reggie knew I meant business, because he stood right up and moved out into the aisle.

"I'm so sorry, Archie," whispered Candy as we got out of our seats.

"It's okay," Archie muttered. As he moved up the aisle, a trail of cola dripped in his wake.

We went into the lobby and surveyed the damage. Archie's pants were drenched. "We'd better go home," Candy said. "Once again I ruined the whole evening."

"No, no," contradicted Archie. "We don't have to leave. I can dry my pants in the men's room. Everything will be fine, right, Reg?" He looked to Reggie for support.

"It will?" replied a puzzled Reggie.

"Come on!" Archie said. He yanked on Reggie's tie and led him away. They disappeared into the men's room, leaving us alone.

"I did it again." Candy sighed.

"Forget it," I answered. "It could have happened to anyone."

"But it always happens to me." Candy was hard to console.

"That's all in your mind," I argued. "Come on. I challenge you to a game of Super Stupor Brothers." I pointed to the video games in the lobby. After we had played a while, Reggie and Archie emerged from the men's room. Archie's pants looked stained but dry.

"They're as good as new," Archie said as he approached us.

"He took them off and used the hand dryer to dry them," chuckled Reggie.

I looked at Archie and smiled. He was sure going to a lot of trouble to please my cousin. I really appreciated it.

"Do you want to see the rest of the movie?" Archie asked.

"I don't think so," Candy answered meekly.

"Why don't we go out for pizza?" I suggested. "I'm starving."

"Reg?" Archie looked at Reggie.

"Okay by me," Reggie replied. "The best parts of the movie are over now anyway. Nobody else is going to get killed."

"That settles it," Archie announced. "Let's go."

We left the theater and walked around the corner to our favorite pizza place. "This place serves the best pizza in town," I told Candy, trying to cheer her up. She was still moping over the soda incident.

"That's right," agreed Reggie as we went inside. "Jughead Jones rates it four stars. And when it comes to food, Jughead really knows his stuff."

A faint smile finally crossed Candy's lips. We took off our coats and sat down at a table. A waitress came over and we ordered a pitcher of root beer and a large pie with the works. Ordering the most expensive pie on the menu was Reggie's idea, of course. He knew Archie was footing the bill.

By the time the pizza arrived, we were having a good time again. We were talking about teachers at school, and laughing about little things that had happened during the week.

"Dig in," Reggie suggested. Archie poured drinks from the pitcher for all of us.

"This pizza is delicious," Candy admitted as we munched on the pie. We finished our first slices quickly.

"Would you like another slice?" Archie asked Candy. She nodded.

"It's so good I can't resist." She lifted her paper plate and held it in front of me for Archie to put the pizza on. He slipped the slice on the plate. The plate bent in half.

"Whoops!" cried Candy. *Slop!* The pizza fell facedown on my white dress. I had pepperoni in my lap and peppers and mushrooms on my knees. Globs of sauce and smears of olive oil were all over my favorite dress.

"The girl is amazing," Reggie muttered, shaking his head. "No one is safe around her."

The rest of us were so stunned we couldn't speak. I took a deep breath and counted to ten. "Don't worry, it's okay," I said through gritted teeth. I was a total mess. "But I think we'd better go." I scooped pizza and sauce from my lap back onto the serving platter.

"Right," said Archie. He and Reggie went over to pay the check.

"It's just not your night," I said to my cousin, who was on the verge of crying. "But really, I'm glad this happened. It gives me an excuse to buy a new dress. This old thing was getting shabby anyway."

"Sure," said Candy in a small whisper. She was too choked up to speak.

The boys returned and helped us on with our coats. There was nothing left to say. We walked back to Archie's car in silence. When we got there, we found another surprise waiting for us, on Archie's windshield. It was a parking ticket. Candy had forgotten to put the money in the meter. Archie tried to be pleasant, but I could tell his patience was strained to the breaking point.

"It's no big deal," Archie steamed as we climbed into Ol' Betsy. "The fine is only a whole week's allowance." He started the car. She backfired twice before rumbling off.

The drive home was even quieter than the walk to the car. The date had turned into a triple disaster.

"You don't have to walk me to the door," Candy said when we pulled into her driveway.

"Candy, do you want . . ." I began.

"No, Betty," Candy said as she got out. "You'd better go home and clean up. I just want to be alone." Candy paused. Her eyes were watery. "Thanks for the nice time. I'm sorry I spoiled everyone's evening." She slammed the car door and ran up to her house.

Archie looked at me apologetically. I sighed in dismay.

"I told you that babe is poison," Reggie said.

Chapter 10

After we dropped Candy off, we drove Reggie home. "Thanks for the lift, Freckle Face," Reggie said when we stopped in front of his house. He turned to me and smiled before hopping out of the backseat. "Do I rate a good-night kiss?" he asked me.

I looked at him sternly and shook my head. "Reggie, you're some piece of work," I said.

"Of course," he replied. "In fact, I like to think of myself as a masterpiece. Now, how about that kiss?" He puckered up and reached for me with both arms.

"No way! Forget it!" I snapped, sliding across the seat as far away from him as possible.

"Knock it off, Mantle," Archie growled as he leaned back over the seat. He glared menacingly at Reggie from behind the wheel.

"Chill," Reggie chuckled, raising his hands in surrender. "I'm only kidding, Dude."

He turned to me again. "Sorry if I upset you." He put out his hand. I smiled and we shook hands. "Well, good night," Reggie said, climbing out of the car. "I can't say I had fun, but this date sure was a million laughs." He waved and walked up the driveway to his house.

Archie got out and helped me into the front seat of the car. He climbed back in and shifted Ol' Betsy into gear. I snuggled up close to Archie. It was the first time all evening that I felt completely at ease.

"Do you want to go right home, or would you rather take a little drive?" Archie asked me as we rumbled down the road.

I cuddled closer to Archie. "I'd like to take a little drive," I confessed. "This night has turned into such a disaster I'd like to salvage some of it if I can. That is, if you don't mind looking at my messy dress a little longer." Archie smiled and pressed the car's accelerator. We turned off the main street onto Willow Road, where it wound its way up to Hamilton Hill. Scenic Hamilton Hill was a great place to do a little stargazing and a favorite spot for young couples to park and chat undisturbed.

Driving along in the cool night air felt good. It had a relaxing, calming effect on me.

"You know," I said to Archie, "I've been thinking." I began trying to explain the thoughts that were whirling around in my head. "We all have trouble with little flaws in our characters," I said. "Reggie's problem is that no one knows when he's kidding, like just now when he tried to kiss me good night. My cousin Candy's trouble is that she lacks confidence in herself and that causes her to get nervous."

"And when she gets nervous, she goofs up," Archie interrupted.

"True," I said. "But the point I'm trying to make is that even though Candy's problem is more noticeable than other people's, that doesn't necessarily mean that it's worse than, say, Reggie always pulling pranks and making jokes."

"I think I understand," Archie admitted. "We're used to Reggie and expect him to be a pain, so we've learned to live with it."

"Exactly," I said.

"And because Candy is a beautiful girl,

we're more shocked when she does something clumsy like dropping pizza or spilling a drink," Archie continued.

I nodded. "I think that's why we've all blown her accidents way out of proportion. Maybe the trouble isn't just with Candy. Maybe the trouble is with us, too, in the way we perceive Candy."

"Hey! I think you're right," Archie said as he parked on top of Hamilton Hill. Then he turned to me and smiled. "And the trouble with you, Betty Cooper,"—he put his arms around me—"is that sometimes you don't know when to stop talking about your cousin. Let's talk about me and you."

I looked into Archie's blue eyes. The moonlight seemed to shimmer and dance on them. I felt like I was having a wonderful dream and I didn't want to wake up! As Archie gently pulled me close to him, my pulse quickened and I tingled all over. I shut my eyes and let my lips press against Archie's. Oh, it was so romantic! I'd been kissed before, but there was something special about that particular kiss. Suddenly all thoughts of Candy's troubles flew right out of my mind. I forgot about the horrible evening. I forgot about the rough days I'd had worrying about my cousin's fitting in with my friends. All I could think about at that moment was Archie and how much I liked him.

"That was nice—very nice," I said to Archie when our lips parted.

"On a scale of one to ten, I'd give it a ten plus," Archie said in a voice just above a whisper.

"Thank you for helping me forget my troubles," I said. "Thank you for everything. You're the greatest."

"Thanks for the compliment," Archie said, "but we'd better head home. It's getting late."

"And I'll need my sleep," I added. "Tomorrow I'll have to call my cousin and smooth over the lumps and bumps of this miserable date."

"Sounds good to me," Archie said. "Maybe next weekend we can double-date again. That is," he added, "if I can get an advance on my allowance. After paying for that parking ticket, I'll be flat broke!" We both laughed as Archie started to drive back into town.

Chapter 11

That weekend Candy managed to avoid answering all my phone calls. She just didn't want to talk. Mom said Candy probably just needed some time alone. She reassured me that Candy was bright enough to realize one disastrous date didn't mean the end of the world. But I wasn't so sure. Mom hadn't seen the look on Candy's face when she bolted out of Archie's car.

At school on Monday, Candy still seemed distant. I tried to get her to talk but she seemed to be withdrawing from everything and everyone, including me. Oh, she was pleasant and friendly enough, but it was all fake.

"I'm the homework hound today," I told her as we walked down the hall to first period.

"Thanks," Candy replied sweetly, "but

I'd better copy down my own assignments."

That's the way the entire day went. Before and after classes Candy kept to herself. During class she just sat there like a mannequin. And she completely skipped lunch period. It was as if she was building a cocoon around herself to prevent any more goof-ups. I was really worried about her. I wanted her to know that I cared about her, no matter what. She could spill pizza all over me, every day of the year, and it wouldn't change my feelings for her.

"Where's Candy?" Midge asked me as we dressed to go home after last-period gym class.

"I don't know," I said. "She's been avoiding me all day."

"Is everything okay?" Midge wanted to know. "Candy has been acting funny. She was on my team for volleyball and just hid in the back."

"It's a long story," I said to Midge. "And knowing Reggie Mantle, I'm surprised you haven't already heard it." I was astonished that for once Reggie had kept that big mouth of his shut.

"If you're looking for your cousin," said Veronica, "she's still out in the gym. Miss

Parker gave her permission to work out on the uneven parallel bars after class."

Midge looked at me. "Is Candy a gymnast?" she asked, amazed.

"I don't know," I answered, puzzled. "It's probably just another excuse to dodge me." I quickly finished dressing and went back into the gym. Was I ever wrong! Candy was on the uneven bars and Miss Parker was spotting her. Not that Candy needed much spotting. She was graceful and coordinated. I couldn't believe my eyes. I watched in awe as she performed stunt after stunt, weaving each one into the next in a flawlessly executed routine. Was that really my clumsy cousin Candy?

Candy ended her routine and dropped to the gym floor in a graceful dismount. "Outstanding work, Candy," I heard Miss Parker say. "In all my years at Riverdale, I've never seen better." Candy nodded and smiled at our gym teacher. She didn't see me yet. Miss Parker did. She walked across the gym floor toward me.

"Betty," she said, "your cousin Candy is one super athlete. She makes me wish our school had a gymnastics team." Then Miss Parker continued past me, into the locker room.

I walked over to my cousin. She was bent over, with her hands on her knees. "Hi, Candy," I said.

Candy looked up. "Hello, Betty," she puffed, out of breath. "I needed a good workout. When I'm depressed, working out sometimes helps me forget my troubles."

"That was some workout," I complimented. "How did you ever get so good?"

"I took private gymnastics lessons for years," Candy explained. "I've always loved gymnastics. It's a passion I developed years ago when we first moved to New York."

"Aha!" I shouted, so loud that Candy froze in her tracks. "I *knew* there was something you were good at. You're a gymnastics whiz! And there is no way in the world that a person who can excel at gymnastics can really be a klutz!"

"I'm only good at gymnastics when no one is around," said Candy. "I'm great in practice, but I've never performed in a meet or anything. If I tried to do a routine in a competition, I'd probably flub it up and land on my head or something."

"Bull and double bull!" I said. "If you can be that graceful when no one is around, you can do it when the whole world is watching."

"Do you really think so?" Candy asked dubiously.

"Sure! It's that old confidence problem again," I stated. "You see yourself as a klutz, so everybody else thinks you're a klutz, too. If you could project that positive self-image you have while you're doing gymnastics, that's how others would see you, too."

We started to walk toward the locker room. "It sounds very convincing, Dr. Cooper," Candy said. "I'd like to prove to everyone that I'm not really a klutz."

"When people see you perform some of those gymnastic feats of yours, they'll know the truth," I said.

"So what do I do?" asked Candy, "give a gymnastics demonstration for all of Riverdale?"

I stopped and stared at the bulletin board in the girls' gym. My eyes focused on a note pinned to the board. "I have a better idea," I said. I pointed to a notice about tryouts for Riverdale's cheerleading team.

Candy read the notice to herself. "Me?" she sputtered. "Try out for the cheerleading team? Are you crazy?"

"Nope," I answered. "I'm not crazy and you're not a klutz. I don't know why I didn't think of this before. Veronica, Midge, and I are all on the cheerleading squad. None of us are as athletic as you are. Candy, you can make the team. I *know* you can!"

Candy thought for a minute. "Making the cheerleading squad would really be something," she mumbled. "Gee, maybe I could." Her expression brightened with hope.

"With your gymnastic ability, you're a natural for cheerleading," I urged. "This is your chance to show everyone, Candy. How about it?"

"Okay, Betty," Candy said without any more hesitation. "I'll do it."

"Great! Come on!" I grabbed my cousin by the hand and pulled her into the locker room. "Miss Parker is still here. We'll sign you up for the cheerleading tryouts this very instant!"

Chapter 12

After signing up for tryouts, Candy and I went back to her house. "Do you really think I have a chance, honestly?" Candy asked me as we sat on her living room couch.

"I honestly do," I replied. "The only person who can keep you from being on the team is yourself. You've got the looks and the athletic ability. All you need now is a winning attitude."

Candy smiled weakly. "What kind of cheer should I do to earn a place on the team?" she asked.

"Now, that's the right attitude," I said.

For the next hour we worked out a really catchy cheer for Candy to perform. Candy figured out the gymnastic moves, I suggested a few flashy dance steps I knew, and soon we'd developed just the right blend of acrobatic feats, dance moves, and words.

"It's a winner," I announced when we were finished.

"That was fun," Candy said. "I really feel good about trying out. I feel . . . I don't know . . . different."

"It's confidence, girl," I said approvingly. "We'll start practicing tomorrow. Mr. Svenson will let us work in the alternate gym after school. That way we can practice in private."

"Are you sure Mr. Svenson will let us?" Candy asked. "He and I had sort of a rocky introduction." Candy was referring, of course, to the water bucket incident.

"Mr. Svenson won't mind," I assured my cousin. "Besides, it's school policy to let students use unoccupied rooms for legitimate purposes."

"Super," said Candy. "I can't wait for tomorrow."

After last-period gym class the next day, Candy and I went to the alternate gym. It was actually just a room at the end of the building about half the size of the regular gym, used mostly to store mats and other equipment for the wrestling team.

Earlier in the day I'd asked Mr. Svenson for permission to use the room, and he'd graciously agreed. He opened the doors for Candy and me and then left us alone to practice.

"Let's get to it," I said as Candy finished her stretching warm-ups. I stood by and watched as Candy went through the routine we'd worked out. There was no doubt about it. Candy really was a natural for cheerleading. She added a few flashy acrobatic twists here and there as she performed, purely by instinct. Her routine simply dazzled me.

"How was I?" Candy puffed after she'd finished her final stunt.

"You were great," I said, "but try it again and this time yell a little louder."

"Right," Candy agreed. She paused to catch her breath and then started all over. Amazingly, the second time the routine went even better. If Candy performed that well at the tryout she would be sure to make the squad. I just hoped she wouldn't get nervous in front of the other girls and the coaches and revert to the old Candy. I didn't think she would. Something seemed different about Candy. Right before my eyes, determination was replacing Candy's bumbling nervousness.

"That's enough for today," I said a while later. "We still have a few more days to practice before the tryout."

"It can't get here fast enough to suit me," Candy said, wiping her sweaty brow.

"Me either," I said as we headed for the girls' locker room.

Secretly, Candy and I worked together every day after school in the alternate gym. Candy worked hard, and her routine got better with each passing day. She never goofed up. She never got nervous. Even Mr. Svenson didn't phase her when he decided to stick around and watch her routine one afternoon. A new Candy had emerged from the old klutzy shell, and it was a wondrous sight to behold. Candy finally believed in herself and took pride in her ability, and it showed.

"How was I, Mr. Svenson?" Candy asked when she'd finished her routine on the last practice day before the tryout.

"Dat vas sometin amazing," Mr. Svenson complimented. "You are one very goot cheerleader."

"Thank you," Candy replied. She turned to me. "Well, Coach? What do you think?" she asked. "Am I ready?"

I nodded. "Oh, you're more than ready," I said. "On Friday afternoon, your routine is going to knock them dead!"

Chapter 13

Candy and I were in the girls' locker room, waiting for tryouts to begin. There were lots of other girls there, too. The packed room buzzed with excitement.

"It's now or never," Candy said to me. "Today I show everyone a new Candy Collins."

"You can do it," I told my cousin. "Deep inside, you know you can."

Candy looked me straight in the eye and then nodded.

"I have to go out into the gym to help with the judging," I said. "The girls who are already on the team help grade the girls who are trying out. But we're not allowed to grade friends or relatives, so I'll have nothing to do with your total score."

"That's fair," Candy said. "But would you tell me again how we're graded?"

"Sure," I agreed. "The two coaches, Miss Parker and Mrs. Matthews, will grade you from one to ten," I explained. "Three cheerleaders who don't know you will do the same. So a perfect score would be fifty. But no one ever gets a fifty," I said. Candy nodded understandingly.

"The girls with the highest totals are then asked back, to compete in a final tryout," I continued. "The ones with the highest total from both tryouts make the team. This year we're adding only three girls to the squad, so competition will be extra tough."

"I'm going to be one of those three girls," Candy said in a way that made me believe her. She'd never seemed so positive about anything before.

"Good luck," I said. I kissed her on the cheek and gave her a big hug.

"Thanks," said Candy. "No matter what happens, thanks for everything."

I went into the gym and sat down in the bleachers, next to Midge and Veronica.

"It's about time you showed up," Veronica said. "We were about to start without you."

"What have you been up to?" Midge asked. "You've been acting strange all week. We've hardly seen you after school."

"Oh, I've been busy," I replied, dodging the question. I hadn't told anyone about the practice sessions with Candy.

"Our first girl is Melanie Martin," Miss Parker announced as a tall, good-looking brunette came into the gym. "Midge, Betty, and Tammy will score her routine. You may begin, Melanie."

Melanie started her cheer. She had a good voice, and she was very enthusiastic. Her routine was also good. She did a few round-offs and finished with a jump into a split. The score of forty she received guaranteed her a return trip to the finals. It was just under the school record of forty-one, which had been set two years ago—by me!

Girl after girl came out to perform routines. Some were almost as good as Melanie but most were not quite up to the standard she'd established. Each candidate was told her point total when she was finished. And so it went until we got down to the last name on the list . . . Candy Collins!

When Miss Parker announced Candy's name, Midge and Veronica almost fell off their seats.

"Candy?" sputtered Veronica. "She can't be serious."

"Betty, why didn't you tell us?" Midge asked.

"Her name was on the list," I said. "Didn't you see it?"

"We never pay any attention to the sign-up list," Veronica said, staring at me. "You know that."

"It won't make any difference," I answered. "None of us can grade her anyway."

"How could you do this to your own cousin?" Midge asked. "It's going to be embarrassing for her. She'll probably get the lowest point total in Riverdale history."

"She might end up with minus points," predicted Veronica snobbily.

"Maybe, and maybe not," I said as Candy took her position before the judges. Miss Parker called out the names of the girls who would grade Candy.

"I can't bear to watch this," Midge said. She covered her eyes with her hands.

I looked at Candy. She looked back at me, smiled, and gave me a slight nod.

"Riverdale!" called Candy in a strong, loud voice. She did a graceful leap and whirled her arms. "Riverdale! Fight! Go! Win!" Candy did a round-off and a series of back flip-flops, then continued her

cheer. She finished the routine with a running round-off into a full front somersault, and a slide into a side split. "GO! FIGHT! WIN!"

There was a second of silence, then a burst of thunderous applause.

"What happened?" Midge cried, uncovering her eyes. "What happened?"

"A miracle happened," said Ronnie. "You should have seen it, Midge. Candy was amazing. She did the best routine I've ever seen."

When the clapping was over, Miss Parker walked out to a blushing Candy. "Candy," she began, "that was marvelous. You have a record-setting total of forty-eight points. Congratulations, and good luck on Monday."

As Miss Parker moved away, girls rushed out of the stands to introduce themselves to Candy and to congratulate her. Midge, Veronica, and I were the last ones to reach her.

"Congratulations, Candy," said Midge as she hugged my cousin.

"I'm really happy for you," Veronica chimed in.

"Betty, I did it," cried Candy happily when she spotted me. We hugged and kissed.

"I knew you could," I said. "I told you so. You're a cinch to make the squad. All you have to do now is knock 'em dead at the finals on Monday."

"I will," vowed Candy. "The old klutz is dead. My mom should see me now."

Hmm, I thought. That sounds like a good idea. "I think it's time we shared our little cheerleading secret with the family," I said to my cousin.

"What do you mean?" asked Candy.

I leaned over and whispered my idea into her ear.

Chapter 14

That night I convinced Mom to invite Aunt Carol and Cousin Candy over for Sunday dinner. Candy and I planned to spring our cheerleader announcement during the meal.

"As usual, the food is wonderful," Aunt Carol said as we dined. "What's the occasion, Helen?"

"Does there have to be an occasion to invite relatives to dinner?" Dad teased. "Back home less than a month, and already she's suspicious of her relatives." He smiled. "I just like to be surrounded by four beautiful women when I eat."

"Actually, this was all Betty's idea," Mom admitted. "She told me she had something she wanted to talk about."

"Really?" said Dad in surprise. He looked at me. "Okay, Betty, talk or else." He pointed a fork in my direction.

I looked across the table at my cousin. She wiped her lips with a napkin and winked at me.

"Well," I began, "I wanted to talk about cheerleading."

"Don't tell me they kicked you off the cheerleading team," Dad said, pretending to be shocked.

I shook my head. "I wanted to talk about somebody else and cheerleading," I clarified.

"It can't be me," Aunt Carol said. "I'm too old to be a cheerleader." She looked at my mom. "Is it you, Helen? You were captain of the cheerleaders in high school."

"It's Candy!" I said, ending the speculation.

"Candy?" repeated Aunt Carol in disbelief. "Candy trying out for cheerleading? Don't be ridiculous!"

Candy shot her mother an icy glance. I did likewise. There was dead silence.

"I mean," sputtered Aunt Carol, "that Candy is too busy with other things to get involved in cheerleading. I was the same way. I never had time for frivolous things like cheerleading while I was in school."

That comment drew the iciest glance of all. And it came from my mom.

"I think it's wonderful that Candy wants to try out for cheerleading," my mom said.

"Ditto," echoed my dad.

"Actually, I've already tried out," Candy announced proudly. "And I made the first cut."

You could have heard a pin drop in the room. Aunt Carol's jaw dropped open and hung there for a few seconds before she could regain her composure.

"That's right," I confirmed. "In fact, Candy got the highest grade ever recorded in the history of Riverdale cheerleading."

Mom and Dad applauded. Aunt Carol joined in, reluctantly.

"If she does half as well in the finals, she'll make the squad, no sweat," I continued.

"When are the finals?" Dad asked.

"Monday after school," I replied. "That's why I wanted us to have dinner together. Relatives are welcome to come to the finals. I think it would be nice if we were all there to watch Candy's routine."

"I'd love to, but I can't get off work early," Dad said. "I'm sorry. I wish I could."

"I'll be there, for sure!" Mom said eagerly.

Candy smiled. She looked at her mom. Aunt Carol took a deep breath and exhaled loudly. "I wish you girls had told me about this sooner," she said. I saw Candy's face fall.

"We couldn't, Mom," Candy said. "We didn't know how I'd do in advance. Can't you please come? It means a lot to me."

Aunt Carol reached across the table and put her hand on Candy's. "I wish I could, Candy Girl," said Aunt Carol. "But I have an important business meeting on Monday afternoon."

"Can't you postpone it or reschedule it?" I asked.

Aunt Carol turned to me. "What would the company think of me if I canceled a business meeting to attend cheerleading trials?" asked Aunt Carol.

"Oh, I don't know," Mom said. I could tell Mom was angry from her tone of voice. "They might think you were just being a mother."

Aunt Carol gave her a dirty look. "Being a single parent isn't that easy sometimes," she snapped. She dropped her napkin and stood up. "I think we'd better go. We don't have time for dessert. Thank you for the dinner, Helen. Let's go, Candy."

"I'll get your coats," offered Dad as he slid out of his chair. I could see he felt uneasy.

Poor Candy didn't know what to do or say. Timidly, she rose. "Thank you, Aunt Helen," she said. She looked at me and shrugged.

"I'll call you later," I said to Candy. I didn't say anything to my aunt. I was beginning to wonder if my aunt was human or just a work robot.

Candy and Aunt Carol left unceremoniously. Mom and I were still at the table when Dad returned from showing them out.

"Same old Carol," Dad griped as he sat down. "Touchy and stubborn as a mule."

"What gives with Aunt Carol, Mom?" I had to ask. "Why is she like that?"

Mom shook her head. "I don't know," Mom answered. "I can't explain why success has come to mean so much to your aunt. Maybe it's because she had so little of it until late in college. Carol was always pretty much of a loner." Mom sighed and then continued. "When her marriage broke up, Carol decided to take on the whole world single-handedly. She's done well, but she doesn't realize she's failing her daughter by pretending to be the perfect career woman."

"Amen," said Dad. Then he steered the conversation to his favorite subject. "Now what's for dessert?"

Chapter 15

On Monday, the school day couldn't pass fast enough to suit Candy. From first period to last, all she talked about were the tryouts. Finally the last bell sounded. The moment of truth had arrived.

"Good luck, Candy," Veronica said as she walked past my cousin in the girls' locker room.

"Right! Knock their socks off," Midge added. Midge and Veronica gave Candy two thumbs up before going into the gymnasium.

"Everybody is pulling for you," I told Candy. "The whole school was talking about your score today."

Candy gulped. "Are there many people in the gym?" she asked nervously.

"I don't know," I answered. "Let's take a peek."

We opened the door that led into the

gym halfway and peered into the gym. There were quite a few people on hand to witness the cheerleading finals. Clusters of parents were wandering in, and groups of students were starting to show up, too. In one section of the bleachers we spotted Archie, Jughead, and Reggie.

"It looks like a pretty good turnout," I said.

Candy exhaled loudly. "I'm a little nervous," she admitted. "I'm starting to think . . . well, maybe I've made a mistake."

"Don't you dare start thinking like that!" I warned.

"I'll try not to," Candy promised.

"Look!" I said pointing across the gym. "There's my mom!" Candy and I waved. My mom waved back. We started to close the door when my mom started waving both arms as if to signal us.

"What's wrong with her?" I wondered aloud. Mom waved some more and then pointed in the direction of the double doors leading out into the hall. We shifted our gaze and saw someone standing by the doors and looking around like a lost soul.

Candy's eyes opened wide in amazement as she recognized the figure. "I-it's my mother," Candy cried. "She came after all. She said she wasn't going to, but she did!"

"Aunt Carol?" I whispered in disbelief. I looked again, just to be sure. "It *is* her!" I started to wave to attract Aunt Carol's attention.

Aunt Carol looked in our direction. When her eyes focused on us, her face lit up like a beacon. She smiled broadly and hurried over.

Candy threw her arms around her mom and hugged her. "Mom, you came!"

"I had to," Aunt Carol said as tears formed in her eyes. "I *wanted* to," she corrected. "I thought a lot about what Helen said the other night about being a mother. I realized I've had things wrong for a long time. Being a businesswoman doesn't have to mean I can't make time to be a good mother, too."

"But what about your appointment?" Candy asked.

"I canceled it," Aunt Carol explained. "If they want to fire me over a dumb appointment, let them. I want to be here when my daughter makes the cheerleading squad."

Candy stepped back from her mom. "Suppose I don't make it?" Candy asked. "Suppose I mess up?"

"If you do, you'll certainly take right after your old mother," Aunt Carol said matter-of-factly. Candy stared at her mom. She couldn't believe her ears.

I knew what was coming and thought it might be better if I left them alone. "Excuse me," I said, planning to join the crowd on the bleachers.

"Stay, Betty," said Aunt Carol. "Please stay. I want you to hear this, too." Aunt Carol looked at Candy through watery eyes. "That story about being too busy for cheerleading in high school was a lie," she began.

"It was?" asked Candy, puzzled.

Aunt Carol nodded. "I tried out for the team two years in a row. I never made it. I was just too awkward."

"You, awkward?" Candy muttered in surprise.

"That's right," said Aunt Carol. "I was a perfect klutz in high school. They used to call me Clumsy Carol. I was a walking disaster area."

I smiled. My aunt's sudden confession had the right effect on Candy. "You used to be Clumsy Carol and you turned out to be . . . to be . . ."

"Not so perfect after all," finished Aunt Carol. "In fact, I realize I've handled single parenthood in a pretty clumsy fashion. But I'm going to start changing that right now."

Candy looked at her mom. "I'm proud that I take after you, Mom," sniffed Candy, wiping away a tear.

"To use one of Betty's favorite words," said Aunt Carol, "bull! I didn't get over my clumsiness until college. You've already outgrown yours."

"She sure has," I interrupted. "And now it's time for her to prove it to all of Riverdale. The tryouts are about to begin."

"Then we'd better take our seats," Aunt Carol said. She kissed Candy. "Good luck, Candy Girl!"

"Thanks, Mom," Candy replied. She went into the locker room and closed the door behind her.

Aunt Carol and I walked over to my mom. "Welcome, Sis," Mom said with a broad grin.

Aunt Carol sighed. "Do you mind if a perfect idiot sits next to you?" she asked.

"Be my guest," Mom replied. "I saved you a seat. I knew you'd be here." Aunt Carol smiled and sat down.

"Come on, Betty," Miss Parker called to me from the judging area. "You're holding everything up."

"I've gotta go," I said. "I'll talk to you after the tryouts." I rushed to the bleacher section where the cheerleaders were sitting and squeezed in between Midge and Veronica, feeling happy and excited.

There were eight finalists for the three openings on the squad. The competition was really tough. Each finalist seemed better than the last. The crowd was buzzing by the time Candy came out as the final performer.

Candy took her place. She looked around. The room was silent.

"Go get 'em, Candy," Reggie Mantle suddenly yelled from the stands. Everyone laughed. Candy smiled. From the way she smiled, I knew she was in control.

"Riverdale!" shouted Candy, her voice ringing through the rafters of the gym. She leaped high and gracefully. "Riverdale! Fight! Go! Win!" she hollered before going into a perfect round-off and a series of back flips. All eyes were riveted on her as she got to her feet again. "Go, Riverdale! Fight, Riverdale! Win, Riverdale! RIVERDALE!" she belted out as she started her run. Candy did another round-off. Sailing high, she did a full forward somersault in a pike position. Her landing was flawless. As she dropped into a side split with her arms raised, she yelled, "GO! FIGHT! WIN!"

The spectators were stunned, the gym deathly silent. Calmly, confidently, Candy held her final pose. And suddenly an eruption of applause came from the crowd—a thunderous ovation for Candy's performance. Across the floor I could see Archie, Reggie, and Juggie yelling, screaming, and whistling. Mom and Aunt Carol were clapping so hard their hands were turning beet red. Even Candy's competitors were cheering. It was the moment Candy had been waiting for for all those years. Candy the nerd, Klutzy Candy, was gone forever. Candy had finally arrived. She was accepted. She was great.

I was proud of my Aunt Carol, too. Like Candy, she'd made an important decision to change for the better. To tell the truth, I felt a little proud of myself. After all I, too, had contributed to the end of the trouble with Candy.

When the applause died out, the cheerleading coaches collected the evaluation sheets and tabulated the scores of each girl. It didn't take long. When the totals were tallied, Miss Parker lined up the girls who'd tried out in the middle of the gym. She thanked them all for their efforts and complimented them on their routines. Then she announced the results of the competition.

"As you all know," she began, "the three girls with the highest point totals will be added to this year's cheerleading squad." A hush fell over the excited crowd.

"The other girls," she continued, "will become alternates and will be considered for the squad if a team member drops out for any reason."

Miss Parker glanced at her tally sheets. "I now have the honor of announcing Riverdale's newest cheerleaders," she shouted. "Each of these girls has turned in an outstanding performance. Riverdale's newest cheerleaders are: Melanie Martin, Charlene Strausser, and... Candy Collins!"

Again, the crowd burst into a wild round of applause. Candy smiled, looked around to where Aunt Carol was sitting, and then ran over and threw her arms around her. Aunt Carol hugged Candy back and started to cry. I saw Mom wipe a tear from her eye as she looked on. Tears started to trickle out of my eyes, too. I guess that's the trouble with Betty Cooper. I'm just too sentimental!

Chapter 16

I joined the group around my cousin as the crowd of spectators in the gym started to dribble out. Aunt Carol had her arm around Candy. Miss Parker was there, and so were Archie, Reggie, and Jughead.

"That was a once-in-a-lifetime performance," Miss Parker was saying as Midge, Veronica, and I walked up. "No one has ever received a perfect grade of fifty before and probably no one ever will again."

"See, Candy," Aunt Carol told her daughter. "Now *you're* the perfect one." Everyone laughed.

"Now, if you'll excuse me," said Miss Parker. "I have some things to do." She congratulated Candy one last time and then walked away.

"In honor of having a perfect daughter,"

Aunt Carol announced, "I'm inviting you all out for soda and pizza, my treat!"

"Now that's a perfect way to celebrate," said Jughead, licking his lips.

"It sounds great to me," I agreed.

"Me, too," said Candy. It was quickly settled. We were all going out for pizza.

At the corner pizza parlor, Mom, Aunt Carol, the girls, the guys, Candy, and I crowded around a table. Aunt Carol ordered four large pies with the works and drinks. (One whole pie was for Jughead.)

After the drinks were poured and the pizza was on the table, Aunt Carol proposed a toast. "To my perfect daughter," she said, raising her glass.

"To Candy," Archie, Reggie, and Jughead all said as they raised their glasses.

"To my sister Carol, soon to be a perfect mom," said my mom, lifting her glass.

"To Betty," said Candy, "the best cousin a girl ever had." Veronica and Midge saluted me with their glasses.

"To Riverdale," I began, reaching for my soda. "Whoops!" I cried as I accidentally knocked over the glass. Soda spilled all over the table. Quickly, everyone scurried backward to keep from getting drenched.

"Betty Cooper," scolded Archie. "You're a klutz, but you're lovable!"

Everybody burst out laughing, except Jughead. He was too busy stuffing his face with pizza.